MW01136301

The Book of Hims

The Book
of
Hims

POEMS

Alisha Lockley

Copyright © 2019 Alisha S. Lockley

All rights reserved. No part of this book may be reproduced in any form on by an electronic or mechanical means, including information storage and retrieval systems, without permission in writing from the publisher, except by a reviewer who may quote brief passages in a review.

For the meek who roar quietly:
My Grandmothers
My Mother
My Sister

Order of Services

In the Beginning

Devotion

Defiance

Delirium

Dominion

Benediction

In the Beginning

Water for Breakfast

(Golden Shovel after Saul Williams: *I Drew a blank*)

Because my stomach can't hold sunlight and *I*
gagged hard on the hour while I *drew*
back my eyelids; because this is *a*
day the Lord has made; I will lie down and be *blank*
 in it. Because I spent teeth *and*
a dance on joy counterfeit and *I*
took a breath while the wind made a joke of it; I *think*
last night I had too much to pray; *it*
tasted funny on my own ears. There I went begging: *May*
being as I "be" get easier. Then may*be*
my being can be legible. Please, read me as *the*
full grown child I am, *best*
dressed as another tired man's blessing in disguise; A *thing*
of freshly burnt scripture. Lord *I've*
given blood tithes with the moon's tide and I'm still just as human as
ever
With my sun-soured stomach and eyes barely *drawn*

Undone

My daddy gave me
these eyes
as a gift to himself

My mama gave me
bronzed wings
more for show
than flight

My grandmama gave me
her hips for swinging
every day
but Sunday
and some days
sour daydreams
to sweeten
my nightmares

The men gave me poems

I learned
to carry books
the same way
queens carry crowns

To be soft
in the mouth

To stitch clean words together
both in prayer and in unreason

To cry slow and sleep light

To keep lead in my eyelids
gunpowder in my throat
ribbon at my waist
gospel in my teeth
rattling in my belly
lace cuffed at each ankle
too much in my hands

Good Lord
I have so much to unlearn

Like the taste of a scream unvomited
Like how to tear even without bleeding
Like how to drown
Like how to swim in wisdom and not get wet
Like how to tremble at communion
Like how to grow old too young
Like how to fall without surrendering my body to the ground
Like how to unbuckle my knees
Like how to beautify my ugly
Like obedience as if it couldn't have been the death of me
Like church door witchcraft
Like saying amen when what it is isn't so
Like lying
Like leaving things unbroken
Like kissing with the eyes cracked open
Like latch key memories
Like perfection

Dead Cherry

How do you throw a funeral for your virginity?

Asking for a friend
who's saving it for daddy's steady arm
at the wedding
should she become a bride
ripe enough for gifting

He says he doesn't sell used cars

Warns she's nobody's 40 acres
should anything pop loose
before the ceremony

Compares it to Christ's pierced hands
let there be a crimson show
to satisfy heavy obsessions
of a red encore

Lack of evidence may
have her returned to herself
if opened before "purchase"

After all
the boys can't bleed
into their rites
the way we do

Do you behead the flowers for stems?

Toss the double standard as rice?

Throw the whole girl away?

What about the body?

Should it be a thing broken into?

Did the 2nd time at 9
without permission count?

What good was the closed mouth?

Roses prick themselves all the time, right?

Does she lie?

still?

to be petaled for pressing
in black books?

Is her name a curse after?

Is she a dry spell?

homesick
for a place that didn't exist?

13

thick browed
barely breathing
2 inches at a time

Boys laugh behind my neck
I flinch at the dip
of their Adam's apples
wishing
to be a song unwritten

2004

When Usher says
he needs a bad girl
I know I am it

Tooted lips all stank faced
like the beat so nasty
the adolescent juju I make
could hurt anybody

I'm breaking every talking door's neck

Twirling my non-existent happy hips in his direction
while he watches my awkward work
from the bedroom wall
where he's hung
arms splayed
like a crucified playa

Holding a glossy paper gaze
to follow each bony movement

Back when I had the whole house to bump in
without anyone to rebuke my freedom
or say how hoochie and fast-tailed I look

But I still get paranoid anyway

Jump at the sound of every car door
slamming across the street

Afraid my parents might
beat Jesus coming back early

I'd peep out the window mid-guitar lick

So, I'd know when
to start playing
the gospel again

Quincy, F

My second first love
blew my hair in his breath
from the backseat window
when auntie and grandma
drove me to him
every few Septembers

Let me climb all his branches
made me wear skirts with blue patches
never left me empty handed

He always gave
bee stung buttercups
vines of scuppernongs
trees full of pecans
rich smoked vanilla breezes
bowls of black berries
neighbors who knew each other
with names that sounded like the creak
in old record scratches

Widows who picked Japanese plums
and made honey drippers
well into the afternoon
all the wandering
I never had to lust for
void of streetlights

I didn't see him at night
never stayed long enough
to see him breakout in stars
but I've heard the crickets say
he was a devastating beauty
after dark

Hiya

We shook
took wing to foot
skirt tail to hand
breezed fluid
the fabric in our hemlines
while risen hymns
lined the ceiling

We were fire-washed and un-magical

Used to be carrying on
well past
the last amen
so long
we thought
we lived
in heaven's basement
where no angry wind
nor devil
could catch us still
where we rocked the temple
full to its brim

Where women snapped
necks back in the holiest of sass

Where grown men crumbled
from the chest down

Where Hebrew hopscotched
off the tongue

Where we stomped
We swayed
We beat
We lept

Early
on those great gettin up mornings
where our grandmothers danced
for every danger left unseen

Where they cried over each of our names

How we knew what it was
to see rain fall from the inside

Where choirs kept thunder warm in palms

The rhythmic kind
that angels dipped their ears in
and wondered
"What strange symphonies were we?"

Used to drink the air by the limb-full

Teeter home undone like tipsy arrows

We were a jumping city of cracked clay

Knew the Lord by the breath of his hands

Could never keep the altar clean if we tried

New testament and old drum

Both ancient and newborn

In this oily wine gospel

You couldn't help but hum
and shake in

Nylon

I hate it

The tightness

The itch

Feels like
slipping into what
snakes leave to rot

Or a march of bull ants
biting up the thigh

Erasing the waist

Drying the fluid walk

The crinkled swish

a fanfare of paper dolls

I used to run them on purpose

Vowed I'd never put on another pair
past the age of 12

Unless they were fishnets
with a back seam

giving ample stretch
and mad switch

Not that barbed stitch
reserved for the frigid
with no intention of running free

Give me silk autonomy

Lay me unbothered in
my own bed
with room to roll around

Lest I go to shouting
with more than what
ghosts would give

To not move the deacons of the house
to do what they "can't help"

Heaven forbid
temptation and I
show up to worship
in the same black dress

with big legs bare
intending
to claim the body
I use
to answer numbered days

Robbing the husband
I don't have
of his winnings

To say what is mine

My Mother Examines My Abundance

On invisible days
when I walk through a house, I once drifted in
as a pinky thin piece of loose twig,

flossing the breeze between each room

She stops me mid-morning stumble
in my Grey T-shirt and Basketball shorts
with a loaded tongue asking:
"Aren't you a little naked underneath those clothes?"

I ask, "Isn't Everyone?"

Raising a brow

Half knowing better

Half knowing nothing

She says,
"Alright, Miss Thang

You gotta be careful
that jiggle can be something dangerous
one day you'll inspire a man to be a man,
and you'll just have to be a woman about it.

I fix my mouth to walk off lips first

Study the spilled lightening from her scalp

Etchings of the unsaid
wrung hushed around her mouth

I read every blessed word

Each God note
Count the rings on her sprawling fingers

See the bent back and bold legs
on the woman I sprouted off

She had to have been something dangerous too

Devotion

Ode to Lenny Kravitz

A not so guilty
pleasure to watch him
strut

Crooning rugged
in spiked leather

I've never wanted
to be a guitar
so badly in my life

water runs
to wine on the
downward guzzle

Ice capped
man carved
out from thunder clouds

All that woke dew
sparkling
makes him
just the right amount
of too much

Put Your Hands on Me

Both

Stumble

From face
to agitated shoulder

To clay rib

Dip the back

Trek softly

Anoint my corners

Silently

Not loudly
or erroneously
as boys have

Playing cocky surgeons
certain of their clinical magic

Make it light

Falsetto the fingers

Make it dumb

Young and clumsy

Stammer thumbs

Let palms babble

Up calf
Over the knee

Sing in scratches

Again

Up the neck

Unzip the fret

Slip your voice inside

and hollow it

deep enough

for me to sleep in

My Masculinity

Gives you pink elephant realness/ Dashes of gun smoke/ Good looks and cinnamon energy/ Flirts for survival sake/ Has pierced nipples/ A mile of legs/ Long fingernails to x mark what air belongs to him alone/ Would be what Shakespeare called saucy/ Wears heels in his bedroom with the curtains locked/ Giggles deep/ Sleeps like a fire unattended/ Paints murals of lattice in his kitchen/ A sharp boy who braids hair on the weekends/ Spreads rosehip petals open wherever he sits/ Swears a held hand feels like aspirin just when you need it/ Bookmarks a hungered whimper in kisses to save his place/ Same way he prays loudly with the whole mouth/ Makes it stick like a second language/ Speaks fluent trash/ Drinks as much hot tea as he can spill/ Grows weary by blackened rainbows hung head low in all his slumbered trances/ Feather tempered/ Doesn't give a dam(n) for his tears/ Fills champagne flutes with them/ Enough to give a toast to 5000/ Lets others taste the woodsy notes of Georgia peaches and dark joy/ Wanders off/ Swings from the back of my throat in a fight/ Nothing contemporary/ With me in the womb at birth/ Skims an elevator gaze up and down the geography of women we pass on spit stained sidewalks/ Finds most of them gorgeous/ And doesn't say a word

He Talmboutsome:

Wuz good baby girl?
You not gon say good mornin'
wit yo fine ass

Don't be scary
I jus wanna talk to ya

You lookin like a good mirror
to throw my whims at

Im tryna be where you come from

Where you goin sugar?

Southside?

You hongry?

I know I am
got this blade for my mouf

Gotta get you one

Can't be walkn' out here
without sharp cover

Gotta cut more than eyes,
 baby

Mess be crazy round this
time of day

What you think about 45?
Yeah, orange inferno

You voted for him didn't you?

Had enuf money at one time

to forget how black you really is

Been baptized in that good green
ain't you?

I bet you still in school too

Damn baaayby
All dat booty and I
can't squeeze no words outta you

Can I ?
…
Don't walk off on my selah
You betta reflect!

You won't know a king
from a poor man
when you see one

Where else you gonna get both
in the same body?

I'm tryna' teach you somethin'

Look here
I eat with blue blood
even if they table too long
for 'em to see me at the other end

Just make me grounded

Aha aha
You prolly like mad quiet inside
like a library

All your words roll together
in caged concert
cause you don't want no random
niggas to break in

Dat's why you keep yo ears plugged
and nem glasses on huh?

I see you though young blood

You look like a smart mirror
to throw my voice at

Take care na

Don't splinter dat pretty pout
biting dem wooden nickels hear?

I got 'bout a million concrete
benedictions to send you on your way

Imma come see bout myself
again

If you here

Have a blessed day

Burgundy Blues On the 7A

We break away

Sway awake

Wade in sun scraps
melted through tinted windows

Serving as plexi
mausoleum to ladybugs

Which dead or alive count
as an omen for the lucky

One woman sits up
rocking

Screaming
all the names of her sons

Running the world wild
with stolen milk

She hasn't seen them since
rehab

She's too much
a baby again herself

She was pretty once
had all her teeth
and mind in place

Loved a musician
so much
she sang away
so many songs of herself

left with us
to stretch
and mourn what dreams
we leave
to smooth pennies
into dollars
and mere livings into lives
we hope to haunt
before we die

Finger to the jagged grain

Bobble heads against
our will

Of course
we can't fall asleep today

Or ever

We may miss our stop

"Florida Man Kills Imaginary Friend and Turns Himself In"

I have so many questions:
Why is it ALWAYS Florida?
WHY???
Did he off a bird with his middle finger?
Was it a fairy starved with unbelief?
A witch he spat on?
Did he choke the flight out of a pig?
Was it a figment of faith in himself he
splattered into shadows against a wall?
If so, aren't we all at least this guilty?
Shouldn't we all live in prisons
if we don't already?

Meet Me

in the moon's shade
in the pastel rain
around half past forever
I'll be wearing my eyes dry
and my hair loose
bring your favorite pair of empty hands
you're going to need them

Leslie

If the Lord ran his tongue
along the horizon's edge
and folded the world in half

Would you still meet me
somewhere in the middle?

Check yes or no

We've been the topic
of angel banter
for years

My mama has been asking about you
ever since Lisa Frank
technicolored our conversations

Back when we dreamed of being old enough
to read poems in Andell's den
with Hakeem
and Que
and Moe
and them

Passing sunsets don't make it any better

They just blush orange and sink

Plant themselves in the night
rolling restless

we never held hands as long as we should've

I'm saving you a seat
next to me on the moon
until we know better

Until every tree lays bare
No matter how many times our inner children grow out of style
I'm still not afraid to be scared with you
Call me when you get this

Defiance

Jackass at the Coffee Shop...

doesn't get a pretty title
or that I choose to be unbothered
at my full table for one
khaki "auraed"
already
smelling of Heineken
and blow up dolls
at 2 in the afternoon

A limp cigarette faints
behind his left ear
waiting to play
tobacco damsel
between his
pinched lips

Jackass musters the dankest
of damp charm to ask
how African my chocolate is
which tells me
this solo conversation
is one measure too long for my attendance

Jackass asks why I'm single
plays an invisible
violin with his hoofs
for pity in jest
before I choose to respond
"because a good girl can't be complete
and alone at the same time"
he says
as if I'm missing limbs

and I now want to punch Jackass
dead in his pierced snout
just to prove I got hands
but it still isn't over
No

Jackass has a lot to say
Jackass's throat is a gold mine
In fact
Jackass is so blithely unaware
 of his "Jackassedry"
that he pauses from his impromptu sermon
On how he keeps bed bound magic for
"girls with baby faces and bad attitudes"
to ask:
 "What do you think of me?"

I think he's the lost boy Peter Pan
never came to save

I think he's afraid of his birthday

That his mama dropped him one too many times
because he looked like a blessing wrapped in a bad habit

I think his eyes are deserts
that maybe he's cried once
but his daddy wrung the last
living tears out of him
to save his manhood
from water damage
and he's missing his salt
I'm not his wombed messiah
So I lie and say
"I don't"

A Root's Aside

It won't matter
which tree
they fall from...

All Apples
eventually
get bitten
roll or change
after air
licks the core
brown
and bees
have the audacity
to leave honey behind
in their skins

Why I Left

1.
There was so much of God elsewhere
in the smack of full lips
in silver overcast
the gossip of windchimes
baptized in petrichor
the color purple
I stayed
missing Him everywhere
and didn't even know it

2.
The choirs claps
could no longer call
the right angels

3.
The fruit of my lips
rotted at first harvest
I sang dead songs
shed tears in grief
disguised as joy

4.
I was born on a pew
and as I grew
the doors shrunk

5.
Men of the cloth
cut from human fabric
forget they bleed blood

6.
The fine line between
hush money and love tokens
blurs and blinds
depending on the genre
of the dark it's
given in

7.
The clasp of my bras
never needed anointing

8.
Faking bliss in bondage was exhausting

9.
Once I danced myself apart so hard
not even the floor could hold me

10.
When it ended
my feet had nothing left to give
and I was just another clay figment
waiting for glory

Preacher Boy

Called me
the backdoor bitch
he couldn't kiss
without saying
his grace first

Preacher boy's sins
always borrowed

Preacher boy's bible's
a glass pillow

He keeps proverbial shards
littered between his teeth

So preacher boy
be preachin'
every time
he smiles at me

Preacher boy
yellow high
prettier
than I am

Boasts knowing

Preacher boy
be jonesin'
off the scent
left from his shadow

Off his own
hot copied wind

Stomps tin psalms
into every mouth
open to him

Plagiarized his daddy's
feet down to the shoes

Slept stepped
between sabbath afternoons
without invitation
to my house
having over spent himself
in the offering

Drips liquid
hallelujahs
in my carpet

Names me miscellaneous

and walks out

to keep it platonically
anonymous

more mannish than man
pleading innocent

Held his laugh wet
in other tongues

Felt unholy
in the water running
out of worship

Needed Jesus more than
mama thinks I do

Bankrupt of good intentions
still can't pay his human dues

Too. Damn. Deep...
and wonderful
Had that high head
that rolled in heaven
of no earthly use

Couldn't tell
himself from God

And yet
I'm the heathen fool

Anthony

Waxed on a perfect love as evolutionary theory

White teeth stolen from star shavings

Skin black butter deep

Devilish class of handsome

Peacock of a man

Liked girls green and

Young enough to bend backwards

Had games for days

Should've waned

Could've stained my secrets

Would've been 17 forever

Had he not dodged the bullet

Twisting for him

Looking to still his heart

Seducing him to death

MC Lightweight

Yo
Sir Spits-A-Lot
All I need is a mic stand
for my 10-minute set

That's it.

Frankly my dear
I don't shit your exegesis
but you try
and call me daughter
loud enough
for everyone hear it

You wanna
invite an entire congregation up my dress
with dishonest questions
drop hinge my jaw
and tell them
you're praying for my spirit of obedience
when I don't eat the bitter banter
from your hand ass first

Nigga

I don't know where that's been

Ventriloquism is an antiquated gig
for which I have too much mouth of my own

No Poets, No Preachers No Mascs

no more self-serving
half asinine doctrines
no bleeding sheets
no tears mined for diamond debris
no heart string musicians

Magicians specializing
in random disappearing acts of guile
need not apply

I'm tired

This position is occupied and swinging

That feminine pill you keep trying to
fill is not your prescription

Darling
just let me be without apology

I can take it to the bridge from here

Brother
you think you speak punani
cause you tried on a couple

Please

Get off my clit

I ain't no joke

This aint no Hottentot costume

I'm not a punishment

I'm not the callous from your feet

The street you piss in
for keeps

The mind you change
to dim in wit
how quick
you forget
obedience school is for bitches

I am no longer the one
for target practice

I'm not about to hold my breath
for a mocking bird or a brass ring

You not about to have me fainting lonely
when you tumbled here

Got your bones dressed
against the satin in our bellies

Stretched us open
to bid you exit and re-entry
just to fix your mouth
right in your face

You who snap us in half
just to squeeze you
out

Somehow
still step crooked
to blame us for
getting damp
in the leak of your pain

Leave the uncertain terms of endearment
on love's changing conditions
at the welcome mat of
some other doll's house

Those oil slick lines
you spit
at 2 cents a piece
don't move me none

Even with the spare tongue you keep
for lying
in case of emergency
small g God complex
having lowercases of
brittle philosophy

Got no place
to fold your hands
when the deed is over
and I am indeed over it

Keep them braille sermons
to yourself

I saw you
running from the last wreck
assuming my genesis
as cotton blank
and manless

All honey soft
barely tragic
just to begin your worst

This song is not new to me
I won't dance to it

Just go

I've been missing your absence

Delirium

Prayers

Now I lay me down to sleep
I vow to dream before I speak
I give my heart as bread to break
My soul will fold my bones will quake

Flesh Muse

Love,
you can't fathom
how I ache to leave myself

Vacant and sterile
as the room
I've dreamed of sitting you in

White walled
with gluttonous light
and no place for small talk

No place for dirty promises
of someday-never rendezvouses

No floors of quicksand
nor sleight of hand

No time for smoke and mirrors
I want you to shiver
in knowing what I know now

I need you stripped of the magic

Your exotic fingers
played and picked
my brain to pieces
like remnants
of hopeful superstition

He loves me

He loves me naught

Love,
I hope you found me
just as beautiful
as you thought me naïve

Sweetheart,
there was a time
I looked back to make sure
that you were
watching me leave

Self-swiveled
perched nerves

My skin
clawed at the masses
for the listening
of your eyes

I even tried
walking in a different language
for you

My hips were
swaying French
as if you barely
knew English

"Si vous me permettez je ve glisser pour vous"
If you let me
I will glide for you

My little counterfeit

My time I've spent

My reality check
and wake-up call

If daydreams
had expiration dates
you would be it
Stamped
and ALWAYS
labeled yesterday

I tried
to keep you anyway

Hope spoiled
and soured blessing

You don't usher me
into drunken stupors

There are
no more explosions

No more supernovas
superimposing beneath my bones

Your words
no longer fall
mysterious like manna

I've lost
the miracle in your tongue

I'm sorry
for this case of
mistaken identity

I tried to make a god
out of you
and watched you bleed imperfect

Love,
my biggest mistake
was dreaming you immortal

Consider this a eulogy

My love

My darling

My wasted breath and journey

My full of sound and fury

You are now free to be my nothing.

No Metal 4s

He sat me down
on his bed ledge

Opened my hand

Slipped the gun in

The cold steel came

He's telling me:

"Relax lady"

My life line gives
a little break

He loads the base
I can't swallow

He took my nail

Hooked the trigger

My heart fell out

He said you need
to know the taste
of how this feels
in case I'm not
around

What We Don't Need

Accidental angels
forced into wings

Preemie ancestors
born from gun pops
and trigger happy
powers that be

another t-shirt
airbrushed
with baby blue halos

A procession
of tinted glasses
running salt

The twisted mouths

The screaming
over handclaps

The homegoing music
digging
exit wounds
6 feet deep to the ground

Another spot in the earth
to keep bleaching
blood diamonds
in bitter irony

To explain
Why we make altars in the grass
Why we never get over it
Why we never have enough time to grieve
What we're so afraid of

The crypt is too thick
We are inhaling concrete
Do not tell me
it's all the same air
We can't breathe

Judgement from the Book of Joshua

Come on now Mrs.

I can't have you in ruins
once family visits

Don't you go dying on purpose
turning to a rose bed unmade
at your own hands

Make the Lord laugh
so hard He can't save you

You don't want to be free

Trust

It's not that serious
I know depression's middle name
I just can't give it to you
It's too contagious

It's not your color

Too expensive
for your palette

You couldn't have it
if it bit you in the dark

You just never had love
sting this good

Daddy knows
you can pray with me too, though

I'll keep your hands tied

Even stamp each line
with "In Jesus name"
for good measure

Don't you want to make it
to heaven on time?

True is as True Does

And so goes the best of my broken business
for the open-heart exhibition

I tend to double-dutch to conclusions

I know what it is to be stuck on stupid
to walk for miles in circles
in the back of my own head

I'm guilty of lethal optimism

Confused shattered beer bottles for amber
oil spills for rainbows in the street
and emptiness for levity

I make the best of broken things

And if you press your mouth to mine
I'll swear it's a kiss

Even if you're just saving my breath

I can't help but translate an ache out of context
whenever your touch comes with such a thick accent

And you misunderstand the way my hands
hold the feeling of being felt back

But it's really over now
isn't it

In the Mourning

After he leaves:
he will not say "I'm Sorry"
he will not turn around
try not to stare
your grin
will smear cold
beneath his shoes
long before it knows well
to find your face again
let it go
he will hold your breath
for ransom
in his back pocket
you will wear his cologne
like a ghost
you will melt into
the door frame
remember the autumn
you went parking
by the riverbank
how he tickled
your ring finger
with an empty gesture
how he said
he'd love for the children
to look "half yours"
your left hand
will go starving
for commitment
you grow indifferent
tonight
your heart
is a lightbulb
flickering before moths
you'll wonder

if you ever
had butterflies
in the first place
you'll still
get dressed for him
put on
lipstick and pumps
leave the house
with the moon
chasing at your skirt tails
the city bleeding heavy
in its amber light and rusted faith
will unfold its arms for you
the men on the corner
nursing broken prayers
off liquid heat in paper bags
will throw what voice
they have left
at your thighs
twist harder
show no mercy
to the pavement
tonight
this walk comes
with a warning label
calculate the cost
of rent in your womb
pass the storefronts
carrying your image
better than his memory
ever could
even they will sit curious
to know where you're going
and when you get "there"
you'll sit half empty

at a table meant for two
fidget with your napkin
stare at the front door
waiting for yourself
to show up
order dessert before dinner
over tip the waitress
hoping karma
will pick up the bill
take yourself home
turn on the radio
to wash off all the silence
remove your clothing
piece by piece
see
there's still gold underneath
look in the mirror
cry into laughing
when you still see God
in your reflection
you will love yourself
like it's expensive
you will lay yourself down
and not feel lost
in the morning
you'll fall asleep
and still be loved
in the mourning
I promise...

Mania

She hides beneath
the window some nights

Scales the wall

Crawls the carpet

Trying to sound invisible

Wears water as perfume
practices the jump in her head

The tongue runs in place
getting nowhere with him
and …

He said he meant to do it
because her chest needed breaking in

Bragged about the paces
he took up and down her ribs

Claimed she should've seen it coming
the same way most dolls
expect a beheading
after being bought
with young hands

She was made for losing her mind

So plush

So forgiving

He had keys to her conscious

Locked the exits to her smile

She's running herself to dust
as a new book of lamentations

A fermented song

She is his favorite bottle of whine
to drink among beasts
and he swears
about how he
never wastes a drop

You, Wannabe

everything
flatline
venom and victim
gravity
here
there
the tongue
the cheek
the taste
its words
graffiti on the mouth's ceiling
the church I run to
on my knees
the scrapes
the sheep
the amens in the corner
pastor and pasture
past me
knotted
so gentle
savored
sparkling reputation
the dust under its rug
the broom
my hands
the sweeping
the sleep I chase at 6
the script
the heart off book
the heart off beat
the ill-fitting dance
the stained glass swallowed
its cracks
the rip down from throat to belly
the gauze interrupting the wound

the blow up
the smash
the boom
…
you can not
cause my explosion
and choreograph
the fall out
How it lands
is how it lands

In Therapy

The office is a speakeasy
I'm supposed to be
too holy for by now

The cross to bear
is parked
in the waiting room

Leaking splintered
hope
all over the floor

I'm not changing gods today

My mouth just needs a better grip
on deliverance for catharsis sake

I've been told the pain is just
decoration
a ritual of cataclysmic
calligraphy

I must dance into the ink
on my own terms
without anyone to show me how to do it

How do I do it?

When my origins
have never seen
what it is to be original

In the beginning
all we had
were words
yelling nails
jutting upward
to hang the comfort
of generational
curses

screaming oracle bones
to accompany
tambourine rattles

I'm here because the
tears are drying too slowly

Truth behold

My bloodline
can't get past the altar
to save their lives

Afraid it might leave their faith
with nothing to soothe

An Angry Wasp

once charged repeatedly
at the glass
I sat behind
aiming for the jaw
until he bounced
and bashed off a wing
passed out
mask down
shriveled in the
drip of his own venom

You never wore parables well

you might want to
sugar your poison

Birth of a Dummy

Push for it

Hold your breath for ten
drops of sweat

Collapse back on the table
burning cold against
your back

The clock is an unwise
double amputee

Zoom in to a head
scratched with black paint for hair

Nearly faint
when it slides to the tile
without an umbilical cord

You've been eating for yourself

Your teeth chatter
like a circle of tiny white drums

You find the promise
you carried
had been fake all along

Opposite of Afterglow

If I had my way
I'd stay buried
in your arms
until my sins fall off
and I can blame you
for making me blameless
but I'm late
for a race with the sun
I must win

Shrimp and Grits No. 5

Wash the greens

Snap the beans

Hum to the pot
until it harmonizes back
in doo-wop simmers

She learned it early
to lace staying power in
salmon croquettes
in gumbo
in honey hibiscus ice-tea
that mango cake

Cut a hole in the ceiling big enough
for her ancestors to look down
to cosign the potency
of her stovetop sorcery

She don't do kitchen alchemy
for anyone she don't plan to keep

If she feeds you Sunday dinner on a Friday night
in a dress too big for her shoulders
the same way her grandmother
used to for her grandfather
she's trying to
grab you by the stomach

Fill it so well
it goes to your knees
until you can't go
anywhere she isn't felt

She's making your plate
to embroider
the essence of her seasoned touch
into your tongue's memory
to keep you to herself

Make you think
those groans you give
came from scratch

You fall asleep
in her lap
fuller than the fattest moon
as she stirs your temple
to smooth the
knots out
even in your yearning

Stacks

Thesis to flashbacks

My mid-summer baby

Left a cadence of lapping
phantom waves
to wash me in his absence

Disembarkment vertigo at its finest

Broad shouldered

Rum shaded melanin

Tall as stilted sycamores

Used to rock me deep
in the canopy of his arms

Felt like surgery

Gave me necessary aches
to take away

Withered my vocabulary
to a bouquet of wild yeses

Knew what he was doing
and what to do it to

Purely anesthetic
to forget
the last love I had lost

Netflix Weather

The devil is busy
beating his wife
for the 3rd time this week

while we're going faceless to the world

Give our regards to Eden

I'm listening at you
play those well rubbed violins out of me

Paint my clay city red

Wiretap my thump and pulse from
a different zip code

Speak easy to my petals
until I melt open under the
trouble of your talented mouth

Got my head swimming sky deep
in leagues of cloud nectar

Unraveling wild
in swarms of flutes flutter

Got nerve
to make my legs stutter
taking me as forbidden medicine
wet in the way you do

While walls ooh and ahh
at our fade to velvet static

The hairs on your neck stand to testify
of our bloom

Singing in choirs of goosebumps

Hands graze stubble grains

Fingers pirouette in the kitchen

We are so gone

and it's so good

I'm praying

God will turn His head

just this once

…again

(Dali)rium

By 2:00 I've dipped my toes into a dream
where I've been flattened paint thin
in a place where the days have no nights for a mate
At 3:00 I sit cross legged on a marble chaise
where Dali is resting his head in my lap while I give him cornrows

He gives me a recipe for absinthe

Says to use 3 sugar cubes to tame the taste

I tell him, "I'm no stranger to bitter things."

I once swallowed my heart whole and it burned all the way down

He calls me melodramatic
but says thank you for the braids

At 4:00 we're barefoot in Oz

Dali rolls a poppy between his thumb and index finger
and lights it against the sun

The smoke dampens his accent
and hooks onto my neck like a question mark without a tail

He asks if I've ever "drank his kind of music."

I say, "No, not yet. I'm too young."

He shakes his head

bends down to rescue
a stray penny from the yellow brick

slips it against the love line in my palm
and says, "When the stars are clean, you will."

I almost say amen

IV U

I'd like to grow on you
the way ivy does
on most ruins
Quietly
Swirling
Unsupervised
Adding character disobediently

B.Slade

sangs houses down

reverbs with an
impossible smile

riffs so clean
and quick each note
reads as
salted jazz
smothered
in pot likker

sopped up
with living bread

makes you want to sit
at a diamond's table
for Sunday dinner
with ancestors
who made it over

voice moves you to
jagged shivers

have you swaying
like three sheets to the wind
pulls deeper
just to have you
strewn again

until all you have
to give is thanks

Pipe Dream

My hands were always quick
to save your face from sinking

You'd rather pull a wrist
past your waist band

Peck at my forehead
about where hoteps
take stabs at the 3rd eye

Ball yourself up in my fist

Say "now"

Cue denial to your addiction
when I'm not in the mood
to be your balance

we can't be trusted to be alone
having practiced
this ugly religion of being
so lonely together
and it's only a matter of time
our end isn't here yet

I've become vocal filler
a fix of ellipsis in the flesh

Your laugh
a muted trumpet
buzzing in my neck

Mock my dead grip
I can't hurt you if I tried

You wonder what it is
I'm so afraid of

Dominion

Table Mannerisms

Taken time is never kept
un-leaked through cupped palms

Mouths always run on borrowed legs

A man can only stay where his heart anchors him

You swear by the falling sky
you know all this

But you're still different
of course

The dust you rose from
was pummeled pearl

You're someone else's daughter

Your mother sung you into being
with dead language

You got tangled in his walk
didn't you

Watched your patience pull
between each exiting footstep

Loved how he wore you clean
around his fingers

You were the tightened bow
he forgot to remember

Remember
how badly you wanted to be his food
and the table he excused himself from
repeatedly for something sweeter and more temporary

Yes
he ate
but what a pity

He was never that hungry for you in the first place

Shadow Man

Funny
how you figure me
to be so empty

heavy as I am

you get "lost" easy

stumble all into
the wrong bodies

confused by
whoever feels soft
enough for pretending

admit to loving
me in different versions

on other women

but can't re-member
the lips on my face

take your own blame

I can't be mad anymore

not even about the baby

just numb

you must've burned her
limbs to keep you warm

had her
memorize the crackles
in my laugh

imagine
my tightness
to a mimic

pressed her hands
into your weakness

made her
trace the path
of my fingerprints

Tell me how
she did half
my work
and inherited
you whole

I got your dust
on the good nights

Guess
you couldn't help it

She was too
new

and I've been
familiar
for too long

you grew a
tolerance
I couldn't compete with

got colder
to the touch

interrupted
the open
legs of living
voodoo dolls
in the hope
I'd feel some of you

funny how now
I'm the only one
you've been dead to

I loved you
so bad
I couldn't see
we were never
worth a resurrection

Browsing Loubou's and Swan Songs

I am not Carrie Bradshaw

Not even Cinderella on a good day

But I am on the mailing list
for what I can't afford
because I believe in seeing things
that are not as though they were

And that a good pair of shoes
can drag the breath
out of him

So long as he can hold a gaze
when I'm going
for a mile
or three blocks

The goodbye
spews up as an orchid
between the concrete
at our feat

I want you to watch the exit
and know how much

I'd pay to leave you
seeing red for a change

Dominion

He took me to the beach
just after the moon hummed
amazing grace
with pinkened cheeks
and blue freckles
over the score
of water crashing

the night perfumed
with honeysuckle gladness

I answered
the shore's altar call
without oil
on my hands
and get lifted

I had never seen
a temple so big
and been so happy
to feel so small

Hallelujah

Reprise of a Glow Up

You caught me out
stained glass
window shopping
for a new reflection

Said my hair was thicker
than what you remember

Told me not to be a stranger

after my heart lost your face
after the red phase

I stopped naming my tears after you

Even they don't know how to fall

'Stripping Nameless for Adonis (a.k.a The Thirst Monologue)

three months
since the last love's exodus
and I still
feel like the sin
he's been delivered from

Here I go
rehearsing solitude
in a café downtown
pondering over tea
bergamot tinged sun rays
piercing through the window
licking a tarnish of cheesecake
from my thumb

My eyes rapture themselves upward
I see what looks like
my next sleepless night
wearing flesh

This pristine
dreadlocked Adonis
in a tailored suit
eyes hazel green
5 feet 11 inches of
Lawd hammercy!
could probably
rock me to sleep
in his pinky
if he wanted to

He hasn't a clue that
I'm wishing
I could be his blood
just so I can
hold the deed
to his life
in my dancing

At this moment
I know
all the wrong things to say
to get me
in the right kind of trouble

I have this urge
to stand up
and say
something slick
like…Hey
your soul's untied

You've got stars for teeth
and I have a craving
for strange galaxies

Come closer
there's more
than what meets the eyes
and my depths are ready
to formally introduce themselves

He calls over the waiter
orders a chicken salad
with balsamic vinaigrette
and I wonder how
he could've missed
my pride on the menu

It's the first thing
above my will
to go unnoticed

I want to say
turn around
and bless me
you bronze ocean wave washed
muse impostering a man

The room is blurring
I am ready to spill
every drop of
my melted measure
between your fingers

In the right hands
my spine is marrowed rosary
these knees fold into origami

I'll be your museum
if you let me feel everything
we wouldn't even have to touch

I'm falling awake
in time to notice
he's standing right in front of me
one hand in his pocket
half chewing on
nervous laughter
and squinting

he asks for my name
and all at once…
I no longer have one

Benediction

Mahogany Tempest

<Insert confessional poem on how I came to love my tempestuous mahogany self despite the grief I've been given to cast out all my good black girl magic here>

I told my skin to keep screaming
I ran out of fairy tales

Praised my red nature
til roses wilted in envy
I went to therapy

Let my head go to the clouds
with the trinity
got sky-dipped
and blocked his number

I walked out loud
talked cracking
quips out of tune
about going on with my bad self

for my grandmothers' sakes
my mama
my sister
and every daughter
I never birthed
Made a revival out of it

Unpacked the knots in my hair
blessed each kink with a verse
on the belt that bit my legs
when I dared to cut them out

Spoke of the churches

All the staccato ribbons
falling out my mouth
with the deacon's knees
in my shoulder blades

Talked about
The summers full of funerals
the ones with amber evenings
where I'd hopscotch barefoot
on scalding concrete

The baptism
how the preacher
called me pretty underwater
how I've been see-through since birth

The boys I loved
with their fickle focus
and their arrogant amnesia
at least they left
everything they broke
for me to re-member

Helped me piece together
the honesty of my name

All the pain
every golden sealed scar
in this body
I've come to know
I own
Amen

Acknowledgements

Lord, for the gift you have given me and for the opportunity to publicly feel/heal. This was a fight to finish but I'd do it all again and again (and I will)

Thank you to my editors and to Kindle Direct Publishing for helping this project come to life.

To Justina, my blunt and brilliant big sister, for being a second set of eyes through the writing process and for telling me the truth even when it hurt.

To Jasna Tomic for providing the beautiful cover art. I can't wait to collaborate with you on future projects.

To the muses who granted me joy, heartbreak, fear, a chest to sleep in, etc. Thank you for the experiences.

To my readers thank you for your eyes and taking the time to thumb through the pages of my heart. This is the first of many.